THE Berenstain BEAR SCOUTS

Meet
BIGPAW

THE Berenstain BEAR SCOUTS Meet BIGPAW

by Stan & Jan Berenstain
Illustrated by Michael Berenstain

Hippo

Scholastic Children's Books
Commonwealth House, 1–19 New Oxford Street,
London, WC1A 1NU, UK
a division of Scholastic Ltd
London ~ New York ~ Toronto ~ Sydney ~ Auckland

First published in the US by Scholastic Inc., 1996
First published in the UK by Scholastic Ltd, 1996

ISBN 0 590 13962 2

Typeset by Rowland Phototypesetting Ltd,
Bury St Edmunds, Suffolk
Printed by Cox & Wyman Ltd, Reading, Berks

10 9 8 7 6 5 4 3 2 1

• Contents •

THE *Berenstain* BEAR SCOUTS
Meet
BIGPAW

• Chapter 1 •
Exciting Plans

It had been a disappointing winter for the Bear Scouts. Oh, they'd had fun. They had gone sledging on Dead Bear's Hill, ice fishing on Lake Grizzly and skating on Farmer Ben's duck pond. But they hadn't been able to do much scouting. They did earn one merit badge. It was for cross-country skiing. That was because the snow was so deep, skis were the only way they could get to school during much of the winter.

But now the sun was riding higher in the sky and the first signs of spring were beginning to show. There was still lots of snow.

But here and there, blue and yellow crocuses were starting to peep through. As all the snowbirds prepared to fly north, their places were being taken by robins and mockingbirds.

There was still enough snow on the ground for Scouts Brother, Sister, Fred and Lizzy to cross-country ski all the way to their secret chicken-coop clubhouse at the far edge of Farmer Ben's farm.

There wasn't any heat in their club-house. So it was almost as cold inside as it was outside. The bundled-up scouts gathered around Scout Brother, who was looking through *The Bear Scout Handbook*. Now that spring was on the way, the Bear Scouts were looking for something exciting to do.

"Here it is," said Scout Brother. "Merit badges."

"Yeah," said Scout Fred. "Let's find an exciting one to try for."

"Hmm," said Scout Brother. "How about Computer Merit Badge?"

"Don't think so," said Scout Lizzy.

"Map-making Merit Badge?" said Scout Brother.

"Not exactly exciting," said Fred.

"Basket-weaving Merit Badge?" said Brother.

"Forget it!" said Sister.

"Hey, here's one that sounds exciting," said Brother. "Rock-climbing Merit Badge!"

"Now you're talking!" said Lizzy.

"That's more like it!" said Fred.

"I can see us now," said Sister. "All harnessed together as we rock-climb up the sheer face of some mighty mountain."

"Wait a minute," said Scout Lizzy. "What's that little mark after where it says 'Rock-climbing Merit Badge'?"

"That's an asterisk," said Fred.

"An aster— What?" said Sister.

"*Asterisk*," said Fred, who read the dictionary just for fun, "pronounced *As-ter-isk: the mark used in printing to indicate a footnote*."

"All right, Mr Smarthead. I'll bite," said Sister. "What's a footnote?"

Fred pointed to the bottom of the page. There was another asterisk with some words beside it. "That," he said, "is a footnote."

Brother read the footnote aloud. "'Bear Scouts earning this badge must be supervised by a qualified adult.'"

The Bear Scouts' smiles turned into frowns.

"So much for rock-climbing," said Scout Lizzy.

"I can see us now," said Scout Sister. "Up to our ears in reeds and straw, trying for that good old Basket-weaving Merit Badge."

"Don't give up on rock climbing so fast," said Scout Brother. "Don't we know a qualified adult who might be willing to help us? Think about it."

The rest of the troop thought about it.

"Of course!" they shouted. "Professor Actual Factual!"

"Right!" said Scout Brother. "He's always climbing up some cliff to collect plants and moss and stuff. I bet he's climbed just about every rock, cliff and mountain in Bear Country!"

Things were looking up. Professor Actual Factual was a good friend and was usually willing to help.

"Slogan time!" said Scout Brother.

He picked up a ski pole. The other scouts did the same. Then, with their ski poles crossed, they shouted, "One for all! And all for one!"

"Do you really think Professor Actual Factual will agree to help us get our Rock-climbing Merit Badge?" said Scout Fred.

"There's only one way to find out," said Brother. "Let's go and ask him."

Pretty soon the Bear Scouts were skiing towards the Bearsonian Institution, which was the home and workplace of Professor Actual Factual, Bear Country's leading scientist. It was a little tricky because the snow was getting patchy. In a couple of places they had to take the long way around.

ONE FOR ALL!
AND ALL FOR ONE!

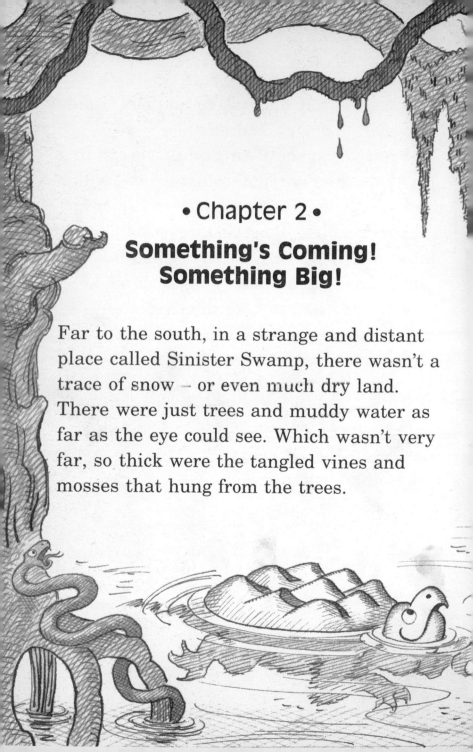

• Chapter 2 •

Something's Coming!
Something Big!

Far to the south, in a strange and distant
place called Sinister Swamp, there wasn't a
trace of snow – or even much dry land.
There were just trees and muddy water as
far as the eye could see. Which wasn't very
far, so thick were the tangled vines and
mosses that hung from the trees.

All was quiet in Sinister Swamp except for the *drip drip drip* of the wet vines, the sound of a frog plopping into the muddy water, and the *splash* of a fish reaching for a low-flying dragonfly. All was still, except for a lizard who was tasting the air, a snapping turtle who was looking for lunch, and a great horned owl who glided down for a snack of snake.

But wait. Something was happening in Sinister Swamp. Something strange. Something frightening. Frogs, lizards and snapping turtles made themselves scarce. Great Horned Owl hid under its own wing. Even the huge swamp crocs, who feared nothing, crouched down low and pretended they were half-sunken rotting logs. It was as though some swamp radar had warned the creatures of Sinister Swamp that something was coming. Something big!

• Chapter 3 •

The Professor Works Things Out

"As I understand it," said Professor Actual Factual, "you want me to help you earn the Rock-climbing Merit Badge."

"That's right, professor," said Scout Brother.

"Be happy to do so," said the professor. "As a matter of fact, I'm planning some fossil hunting in the mountains. So your timing is excellent.

"Now, if you'll excuse me, friends, I must be getting back to my office. I have a great deal to do!"

"But, professor," said Scout Sister. "You *are* in your office."

The professor looked around. "So I am! So I am!" he said. "My goodness! It *is* a mess, isn't it? Well, you just bring me a note from Scout Leader Jane – and how *is* that dear sweet person? – and we can begin fitting you out for rock-climbing gear."

"Er – that's another thing, professor," said Brother. "Scout Leader Jane might be a little nervous about our going for the rock-climbing badge. It might help if you talk to her about it."

"Fine," said the professor, reaching for the phone. "I'll call her right now."

"Why don't you wait 'til the party?" said Brother. "You'll both be there."

"Party?" said the professor. "What party?"

"This one," said Scout Lizzy, who had fished an invitation out of the jumble of post on Actual Factual's desk.

"Ah, yes!" said Professor Actual Factual.

"Readings by Grizzly Gran. Nonsense, of course. But charming nonsense."

It was settled. The professor would work things out with Scout Leader Jane. The Bear Scouts said goodbye, got back on their skis and headed home.

• Chapter 4 •

Much, *Much* Bigger Than the Average Bear

Meanwhile, back in Sinister Swamp, fear was in the air. Something was coming! Something big! But what was it?

Whatever it was, the thunder of its mighty footsteps could be heard in the distance — and felt. The whole swamp seemed to shake as it pounded closer and closer.

To the pounding footsteps, add the crackle and crash of undergrowth and thicket, even trees, being torn away. When at last it broke through the tangled wilderness of tree and branch, the swamp creatures couldn't believe what they saw. It was a bear. But what a bear! A *monster* of a bear! Much, much, *much* bigger than the average bear. Feet like hay bales. Shoulders like boulders. And arms that just *didn't* end! And at the ends of those arms: *BIG PAWS!* One of these paws tore at the tangle. The other held a club the size of a small tree. *Correction*. It wasn't a club at all, but some sort of great log banjo.

As the gigantic banjo-carrying bear moved through the forest, he began to sing. As he sang, he strummed. And so, strumming and singing, he told one and all who he was and what he was about.

YOU CAN HAVE YOUR
SASQUATCH,*
YOUR A-BOM-IN-A-BLE SNOW-
MAN,*
MY NAME IS BIGPAW,
I'M BIGGER THAN 'EM ALL!

ONE THING I LIKE TO DO IS EAT.
AND WHEN I EAT,
I CHOMP AND CHAW,
AND GRIND AND TEAR,
AND RIP AND CLAW!

SO REMEMBER MY NAME,
MY NAME IS BIGPAW!

  * Sasquatch: hairy creature said to live in the
Olympia mountains of the United States.
  * Abominable snowman: hairy creature said to
live in the Himalayan mountains of central Asia.

The swamp creatures watched him tear off a tree branch and chew it up as if it were a stalk of celery. He was something to see, this giant bear who shook the very air with his strumming and singing. Frogs, lizards and turtles watched from their hiding places. Great Horned Owl cracked open an eye and stared. Even half-sunken rotting logs opened their yellow eyes and took in the show.

YOU CAN HAVE YOUR SASQUATCH,
YOUR A-BOM-IN-A-BLE SNOWMAN,
MY NAME IS BIGPAW,
I'M BIGGER THAN 'EM ALL!

SOMETHING ELSE I DO IS DANCE,
AND WHEN I DO,
I WHOMP AND TROMP,
I POUND THE GROUND,
AND SHAKE THE SWAMP!

SO REMEMBER MY NAME,
MY NAME IS BIGPAW!

As good as his word, the great creature not only shook the swamp, he left all the swamp creatures badly shaken. They'd remembered his name, all right. As the giant bear crashed out of sight, they all breathed a sigh of relief.

• Chapter 5 •

Grizzly Gran Does Her Thing

The Bear family and their neighbours welcomed spring each year with a street party. The road between the Bear family's tree house and Farmer Ben's farm was closed to traffic. Banners were stretched across the road, and party balloons were tied to fence posts. It was a covered-dish party. All kinds of Bear Country goodies were brought by the guests. It was a friendly party, with folks getting back in touch after a long hard winter. Farmer and Mrs Ben were chatting with Mama and Papa Bear. Even Chief Bruno and Ralph

Ripoff, who didn't always get along, seemed to be getting along.

"What's *he* doing here?" said Farmer Ben.

"I'm afraid Papa invited him," said Mama.

"Ralph's not so bad," said Papa. "He's got some good ideas."

"The trouble," said Mama, "is that most of them are crooked."

"Well, I just don't trust anybody who wears a straw hat and spats," grumbled Farmer Ben.

The Bear Scouts had had their share of run-ins with Ralph. But at the moment, they were much more interested in the talk that was taking place between Scout Leader Jane and Professor Actual Factual.

"Do you think Scout Leader Jane will go along with our rock-climbing idea?" said Scout Lizzy.

"My guess is yes," said Scout Fred. "The professor can wrap Scout Leader Jane around his little finger."

"I don't know about little fingers," said Scout Brother. "But the professor is giving us a 'thumbs-up'."

"Excellent!" said Scout Fred.

"Great Grizzly Mountains, here we come!" said Scout Sister.

The Bear Scouts were feeling good. They were on their way to a really big-time merit badge. It felt like slogan time. But the scouts never did their "all for one" slogan in public. So they quietly exchanged low fives. Then they joined the rest of the guests. Papa was about to make an announcement. He climbed up on a stump and called out over the party chatter,

"Come close, friends,
and welcome spring!
Watch Grizzly Gran
do her thing!"

Grizzly Gran's "thing" was fortune-
telling. Gramps liked to tease her about it.
"Yep," he liked to say, "Gran'll read anything: crystal balls, palms, tea leaves, left-
over mashed potatoes, dust devils under
the bed – anything!" Which wasn't exactly
true, but almost. Her favourite thing to
read was a dripping, honey-rich honeycomb. And her favourite time to read it
was at the spring party.

The guests gathered round. They looked
forward to Gran's readings. They knew it
was all in fun. But sometimes she got
things right. Like the time she predicted
that Bess, Mizz McGrizz's old hound dog,
would have septuplets. "If you predict
enough stuff," pooh-poohed Gramps, "you're

bound to get something right." Maybe so. But there was an air of excitement as everybody, including the Bear Scouts, gathered close.

Everything was ready. Papa had Mama's big black frying pan. Mama held a bag of flour. Papa placed the frying pan on the stump. Mama sprinkled flour into the pan until its bottom was white. Gramps tied a piece of string to the honeycomb.

It may have been all in fun, but even Professor Actual Factual watched closely as Gran held the dripping, dribbling honeycomb over the frying pan. Ever so gently, she let it swing to and fro, round and round over the flour-coated pan. As she did so, she said in her spookiest fortune-telling voice:

Then *poof!* Gran blew as hard as she could. The flour that wasn't stuck to the pan made a great cloud. Since Gramps was closest, most of the flour got on him. The Bear Scouts laughed. "You look like a ghost, Gramps," said Scout Sister.

But it was Gran, staring at the flour left in the pan, who looked as if she had *really* seen a ghost. Because there in the frying pan was a giant flour footprint. Gran

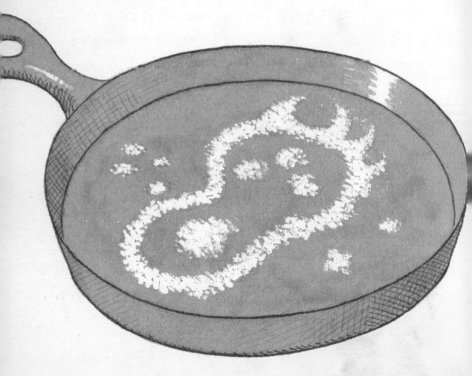

stared at it as if it were the last thing she wanted to see. "The sign of Bigpaw!" she gasped. Then she added, in a frightened whisper, *"And he's heading this way!"*

"Oh, dear!" said Mama.

"Impossible!" said Papa.

"Gracious!" said Mrs Ben.

"If he shows up at my place, I'll be ready with a loaded shotgun," said Ben.

"Now, Ben," said Chief Bruno. "I'll have no taking the law into your own hands."

"I must gaution you, Cran – er, caution you, Gran," said the mayor, who had a way of getting the fronts and the backs of his words mixed up, "a prediction like that could pause a canic – er, cause a panic!"

"Can't help that, Mr Mayor!" said Gran. "Goodness! Don't you think I'd rather predict septuplets or a good corn crop if it was up to me? But it's not up to me. I gotta call 'em as I see 'em. Predictin' gives me an appetite. Come on, Gramps. Let's put on the feed bag."

The crowd began to drift towards the food table. The Bear Scouts found themselves next to the professor. "It's all set," he said. "Be at the Bearsonian tomorrow morning for your first rock-climbing lesson."

"We'll be there," said Scout Brother. "And thanks for working things out with Scout Leader Jane. But I have a question, professor: *What the heck is Bigpaw?*"

The professor chuckled. "No disrespect to your grandmother, of course. But it's pure superstition. There is not, never was, and never will be any such thing as Bigpaw. On second thoughts, let me change that: Take out 'never was'. But come! Let us put on the feed bag – er, let us seek refreshments."

• Chapter 6 •

A Cave with a View

Mountain goats were very much at home
on the rocky ledges of Table Rock
Mountain. The tough, sure-footed mountain
goats lived comfortably on its high, narrow
ledges. The mountain gave them everything they could want: grass and moss
when they were hungry, ice and snow
when they were thirsty, and a view money
couldn't buy.

And early one spring afternoon, it gave
them the shock of their lives. When the
sure-footed mountain goats saw Bigpaw,
they almost lost their footing. Goat mouths

fell open. Goat eyes opened wide. Goat beards trembled.

Up the mountain he came, and up the mountain he went. The great monster of a bear climbed the mountain as easily as a cub climbs a jungle gym. Up, up he went with his log banjo slung over his shoulder. He climbed until he came to a broad ledge, just under Table Rock.

A cave opened on to the ledge. Bigpaw looked into the cave. He had come a long way. He was very tired. He unslung his banjo. He stood on the ledge and looked out over the valley. It was very beautiful in the afternoon sun. Bigpaw stretched. As he stretched, he yawned. Just as Bigpaw was mighty, so were his yawns. They echoed through the valley like thunder. Then Bigpaw entered the cave and went to sleep.

• Chapter 7 •

Tell Us More About This Bigpaw, Professor

The rumble of Bigpaw's yawns echoed across the valley. It reached the Bear family's street party. It was refreshment time. Farmer Ben was in the food line with Actual Factual and the Bear Scouts. Ben looked up. "Not a cloud in the sky and we're getting thunder," he said. "But it's kinda early for a thunderstorm. Wouldn't you say so, professor?"

"I'd say so, Ben," said the professor. Actual Factual knew better than to discuss weather with him. Being a farmer,

Ben had strong opinions about it.

"You'd think Gran would have predicted something useful. Like the weather," said Ben. "Instead of that foolishness about Bigpaw. Why, that story's been kickin' around for years and he ain't never showed up yet. I'll take my pitchfork to him if he ever shows up around my place."

The line had moved, and it was Farmer Ben's turn at the food table. He loaded his plate with goodies. When Actual Factual and the scouts reached the food table, they did the same. They saw a good place to sit across the yard. It was a special bench that Papa had built around a big oak tree.

"Professor," said Scout Brother when they were settled. "Would you tell us more about this Bigpaw?"

"There's nothing to tell," said the professor. "Bigpaw is a myth, he doesn't exist. Let me explain." The professor took a pickle from his plate. "See this pickle? It exists. It's real." He smelled the pickle. "It has a smell." He took a bite of the pickle. "It has a taste . . . mm, it's delicious! Crunchy!" He took another bite, and another and another, until the pickle was gone. "So you see," he said as he wiped his fingers on his napkin. "The pickle has gone. It no longer exists. It is extinct."

"You mean," said Scout Fred, "that there used to be a creature like this Bigpaw, and now it's extinct?"

"As it happens, my friend, you are exactly right. You see," said the professor, "even the most far-fetched ideas are usually based on something."

"Where does the idea of Bigpaw come from?" said Scout Sister.

"From the giant prehistoric cave bear," said the professor. "A creature that has been extinct for nine million years."

"Wow!" said Scout Brother.

"Gee!" said Scout Fred.

"How about that!" said Scout Lizzy.

The scouts fell silent. They were thinking about what a long time nine million years was.

"This Bigpaw," said Scout Brother. "Was he big?"

"Huge," said the professor.

"Where did he live?" said Scout Sister. "Before he got extinct, that is."

The professor got a far-off look in his eyes. "That's what's so strange about Gran's prediction," said the professor. "He lived right around here."

• Chapter 8 •

A Treasure Beyond Price

The party hadn't been a success for Ralph
Ripoff, Bear Country's leading crook and
swindler. At least, not so far. Ralph was
having a good enough time. He'd passed
the time of day with his great and good
friend, Mayor Horace J. Honeypot. Ralph's
friendship with the mayor had come in
handy before and would again. He had
been charming to Lady Grizzly. It was all
he could do, upon kissing her hand, to keep
from taking out his jeweller's glass and
inspecting her diamond bracelet.

But being on his good behaviour was

making Ralph nervous. There wasn't much he could do about it. The food was free, and the balloons weren't worth stealing. Picking pockets was out of the question because Chief Bruno was watching him like a hawk.

After a visit to the food table, Ralph noticed Actual Factual and the Bear Scouts sitting on the oak tree bench. They had their heads together as if they were talking about something really important. Why don't I join them, thought Ralph. I might hear something interesting.

Ralph moved through the shadows and joined Actual Factual and the scouts – on the other side of the bench, of course. What Ralph heard was "interesting" beyond his wildest dreams. This is what he heard:

"Would they be valuable?" said Scout Brother in a hushed voice.

"Valuable?" said Actual Factual. "They'd be a treasure beyond price. More precious than diamonds and gold! The find of the century!"

The words "valuable", "treasure", "diamonds and gold" and "find of the century" rang in Ralph Ripoff's greedy ears like a glorious bell. The party hadn't been a failure after all. It had been a great

success. Who needs to pick pockets when you can rip off a fabulous treasure of diamonds and gold? He had to find out where the treasure was hidden, of course. But that shouldn't be hard. Surely there was a map.

Indeed, there *was* a map. A map showing exactly where Actual Factual hoped to find the fossil remains of the giant prehistoric cave bear. That was the treasure the professor and the Bear Scouts had been talking about.

It was all Ralph could do to keep from leaping up and kicking his heels together. But he sat quietly, hardly breathing, until Actual Factual and the scouts got up to leave. He listened hard for more about the treasure. All he heard was something about rock climbing and meeting behind the Bearsonian the next morning.

• Chapter 9 •
"X" Marks the Spot!

"There's still something we don't understand, professor," said Scout Brother. When the Bear Scouts arrived early that morning, the professor had all sorts of rock-climbing gear laid out in the Bearsonian car park.

"What's that?" said the professor.

"Well," said Scout Brother. "We thought that the way to find fossils was to dig for them."

"That's usually the case," said the professor.

"But you said we're going fossil hunting in the *mountains*."

"Yes. On Table Rock Mountain, to be exact," said the professor. "Let me explain. It all has to do with changes which have taken place in the earth over millions of years. Many parts of the earth which are now covered by great oceans were once vast deserts. Other parts that are now great mountain ranges used to be swampy lowlands."

"How did all that happen?" said Scout Fred.

"In all kinds of ways," said Actual Factual. "You see, the centre of the earth is a great white-hot ball of melted rock. That causes pressure. Sometimes that pressure causes volcanoes and earthquakes. It pushes up great mountains."

Suddenly Scout Sister, who was a bit of a smarty, bent her knees and looked around the parking lot as if she were scared.

"OK, Sis," said Brother. "What's this all about?"

"I'm getting ready to jump out of the way," said Sister, "in case some mountain pushes up through the car park."

Her fellow scouts groaned. But the professor laughed. "Anyway," he said. "To cut a long story short, my studies show that the lowlands where the giant prehistoric cave bear lived nine million years ago are now none other than the Grizzly Mountains. As a matter of fact, I've pinpointed Table Rock Mountain. Therefore, we shall climb instead of dig."

"I can dig that," said Scout Sister.

This time the professor joined the others

in a groan. "And speaking of climbing," he said. "It's time to start your climbing lesson . . ."

A distance away, high up in a tree, Ralph was watching the lesson through powerful binoculars. It was clear that the treasure he had overheard the professor and the scouts talking about was hidden somewhere in the mountains. But where?

The tree wasn't exactly an easy chair. Ralph had a crick in his neck, an ache in his back and a cramp in his leg. He was about to climb down from the tree. But something happened that made Ralph forget about the crick, the ache and the cramp. Actual Factual had stepped into the Bearsonian. A moment later, he came out with a folded piece of paper. He unfolded it and placed it on the ground. It was the map! The Bear Scouts gathered round. Ralph tried hard to read it through the binoculars. But all he could make out was a big "X". The "X" that marked the spot where the treasure was hidden!

Ralph knew what he had to do. His plan called for a very dark night, some skeleton keys and an after-closing tour of the Bearsonian.

• Chapter 10 •

A Dark and Moonless Night

All was dark in the Bearsonian as Ralph came out of the bushes and tiptoed up to the front door. It was a dark and moonless night. Just the sort of night he had been waiting for. It couldn't be better. Ralph had kept watch on the Bear Scouts' rock-climbing lessons. Those pesky scouts took to rock-climbing like ducks to water. It was pretty clear that Actual Factual and the Bear Scouts would be going after the treasure soon. Ralph was determined to beat them to it. He had learned quite a lot about rock-climbing from watching the

47

scouts practise on the small cliff behind the Bearsonian.

He got out his skeleton keys. The third one worked. He slowly pulled the door open, hoping it wouldn't squeak. It didn't. Ralph had been to the Bearsonian a few times and had an idea where the professor's office was. He was pretty sure that was where the map would be.

The Bearsonian, which was kind of spooky even in daylight, was *very* spooky at night. Especially after closing, for some-body who had no business being there. Ralph peered into the darkness as he tip-toed through the museum's great halls. Even machines like old-fashioned steam engines and horseless carriages looked like monsters. And it was really scary moving among the great dinosaur skeletons.

But it was in the Hall of Fame, with its wax statues of famous bears of history, that Ralph got his worst scare. As he

moved among the statues of Queen
Elizabear, Genghis Bear and Blackbear the
Pirate, a light suddenly flashed up ahead.
It was the professor coming out of his
office. He was coming right towards Ralph.
Think fast, Mr Ripoff, thought Ralph. He
stepped up on to an extra stand and posed
like a wax statue. He held his breath until
Actual Factual was long past. Then he let
it out with a whoosh.

When he was sure it was safe, he
stepped down from the stand and moved to

the door of the office. He got out his skeleton keys. But the door wasn't locked. He slipped in, closed the door and put on the light. The map didn't take much finding. It lay right on Actual Factual's worktable. The "X" that marked the spot almost jumped out at him. How foolish of the professor to leave a valuable treasure map out where anybody could find it. Even better, the spot marked "X" was none other than a certain cave on Table Rock Mountain. Quickly, Ralph made a copy of the map on the professor's photocopying machine.

Table Rock Mountain was only a couple of kilometres from Beartown. Ralph knew it well. He'd scramble up old Table Rock Mountain like it was a stepladder. Grab that treasure and nobody in Bear Country would be the wiser. But Mr Ralph Ripoff would be much, much richer. Ralph was so pleased with himself that he gave himself a big hug.

• Chapter 11 •
The Big Climb

Actual Factual's Sciencemobile was bump-
ing and grinding up the back road to Table
Rock Mountain. Scout Brother was in the
front seat with the Professor, who was
driving. Scouts Sister, Fred and Lizzy were
in the back seat, studying the professor's
map of mountains. The Sciencemobile was
a special van that the professor had fitted
out for scientific work. There were picks
and shovels for digging, snorkels for under-
water study, a mini-laboratory for doing
tests, and a telescope was built into the
roof for studying the skies. And, of course,

there was rock-climbing gear for the big climb.

"Professor," said Scout Brother, "I'm still not clear on why you're so sure you're going to find fossils of the prehistoric cave bear on Table Rock Mountain."

"I can't be sure, of course," said the professor, "because there are no sure things in fossil hunting. But to answer your question, I'm very hopeful about the cave marked on the map, because I've been finding shell fossils up there."

"*Shell fossils* in the *mountains*?" said Scout Sister. "That doesn't make sense!"

"It does," said the professor, "if you remember what we were talking about the other day."

"You mean about mountains pushing up out of oceans and stuff?" said Scout Lizzy.

"Exactly," said Actual Factual. "And I didn't just find shell fossils. I've been finding fossils of ferns and water insects.

Which proves that these weren't mountains millions of years ago. This was all low swamp. Just the sort of place that was home to shellfish, water insects and . . ."

"*Giant prehistoric cave bears!*" said Scout Sister.

"Perhaps," said Actual Factual.

"Like, wow!" said Scout Sister.

"Outstanding!" said Scout Fred.

"Totally awesome!" said Scout Lizzy.

"I have another question," said Scout Brother.

"Yes," said the professor.

"Why did we take all those rock-climbing lessons," said Scout Brother, "if we're going to *drive* up Table Rock Mountain?"

"You'll be climbing soon enough," said the professor, pulling to a stop on a rocky ledge.

When the scouts climbed out of the Sciencemobile, they were startled to see they were already more than halfway to the top of the mountain.

"This is my secret 'back-door' route. Before I found it, I used to climb the front face of the mountain. It's a very hard climb," said the professor.

"Look!" shouted Scout Lizzy. "We've got company!" She pointed to some mountain goats on a narrow ledge across the way.

"*We* don't have company," said Actual Factual with a smile. "*They* have company.

Amazing animals. Been studying them for years. It's thanks to the mountain goats that we're up here." The Bear Scouts were already wearing their climbing harnesses. The professor was snapping safety lines on to them. "It was during my mountain goat study that I started finding these strange fossils. It was a case of pure serendipity."

"Seren-whoozy-whatsis?" said Scout Sister.

"Definition please, Fred," said the professor.

"*Serendipity*," said Fred. "Pronounced *ser-en-DIP-i-ty: the finding of something of value by accident*."

"You mean like if you're picking dandelions and you find a four-leaf clover?"

"Correct," said the professor. "Now, here's our climbing plan: We're not going to climb directly to the cave, which is on the face of the mountain. We're going to climb to Table Rock."

The scouts looked up at the strange rock formation called Table Rock. It was a little scary-looking. The great flat rock was balanced on the mountain's sharp peak.

"Gee, professor," said Scout Brother. "It looks like it might tip over easily."

"No fear of that," said Actual Factual with a chuckle. "It would take a lot more than four Bear Scouts and a skinny professor to tip that rock over. Been balanced up there for millions of years, and it'll stay up there for millions more. In any case, we'll climb to the top. We'll reach the cave by lowering ourselves down the other side. The main cave is just below Table Rock."

The professor began hammering in
spikes for the scouts to hook their safety
lines to. He climbed higher and higher,
driving spikes into the mountain as he

went. The scouts followed behind him. As they climbed, they shifted their safety lines to higher sets of spikes.

"What about you, professor?" called Scout Brother. "You don't have any safety lines!"

"Don't need 'em!" said the professor. "Forgive me for bragging. But I may just be the most expert rock climber in Bear Country."

He certainly seemed to be. He found footholds and handholds where there didn't seem to be any. As he climbed up the mountain, driving spikes as he went, he seemed as sure-footed as his friends the mountain goats.

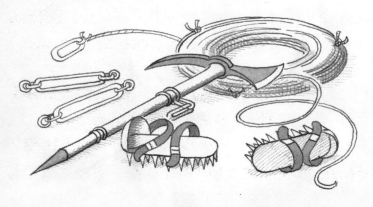

• Chapter 12 •

Oops!

When the Bear Scouts reached the top of
Table Rock, the first thing they did was
enjoy the view. It was spectacular! As they
looked out over the valley, they were filled
with pride in what they had done. They
could see Beartown far below. They could
pick out their homes, Bear Country School
and the Bearsonian. They could even see
the smog from Big Bear City in the
distance. Though they still hadn't reached
their goal – the cave below Table Rock –
they had earned the Rock-climbing Merit
Badge many times over.

"If only our parents could see us now," said Scout Brother.

"And Gramps and Gran," said Scout Sister.

"And Scout Leader Jane," said Scout Fred.

"And our friends at school," said Scout Lizzy.

"And so they shall!" said Professor Actual Factual. "That's why I brought my camera." He took his camera out of its case and looked into the viewfinder.

"OK, now. Move closer together," said the professor. He didn't have to ask the Bear Scouts to say "cheese" because they were already grinning like Cheshire cats. "Closer, so I can get you all in the picture," said the professor, backing up a bit.

Scientists are often said to be absent-minded. But the problem with scientists – and Actual Factual was Bear Country's greatest scientist – is not that they are *absent-minded*. The trouble is that they focus so hard on the problem of the moment that they forget to be careful. The professor's problem of the moment was getting all the scouts into the picture. So he kept backing up until he backed right off the edge of Table Rock.

"Professor!" screamed the scouts. Their smiles turned to looks of horror as they rushed to peer over the edge of Table Rock. But instead of seeing the awful thing they expected – the sight of Actual Factual bouncing down the mountainside like a rag doll – they saw something much more shocking. A great hairy arm had reached out and caught the professor in a huge paw. The scouts stared in disbelief as the arm, the paw and the professor were pulled back into the cave.

As one, the Bear Scouts remembered Gran's prediction.

"Bigpaw!" they said.

• Chapter 13 •
A Chilling Sight

The Bear Scouts were in shock. They wouldn't have been surprised if bits and pieces of the professor had come flying out of the cave.

"Poor Professor Actual Factual!" wailed Scout Lizzy.

"We have to do something!" cried Scout Sister.

"Yes," said Scout Fred. "But what?"

"It's very simple," said Scout Brother. "We have to go down there and rescue him."

"Rescue him?" said Fred. "Did you see that giant hairy arm?"

"And that paw?" said Lizzy. "It was as big as a skip!"

Scout Brother leaned over the edge of Table Rock. "Here's what we'll do," he said. "There's a ledge off to the side of the cave. We'll take off our safety lines, tie them to one of these rocks and shin down to the ledge."

But his fellow scouts just stood there looking scared.

"Look," said Brother. "I know you're scared. We're all scared. We'd be stupid not to be. But being brave when you're scared is what being brave is all about. Now, come on!"

The scouts shinned down to the ledge.

"So far, so good," said Brother.

"So far, so nothing," said Fred. "Shinning down is one thing. Going into that cave is another."

The scouts flattened themselves against the mountain and inched towards the mouth of the cave.

"We came here looking for cave bear fossils," said Scout Sister. "I'm afraid the only bones we're going to find are the professor's."

"D-don't say things like that," said Scout Lizzy. "It g-gives me the shivers."

"Sorry," said Scout Sister.

They had reached the cave.

"I can't hear any growls or groans," said Fred.

"Or any crunching of bones or grinding of teeth," said Sister.

"Stop *saying* those things!" said Lizzy.

"Sorry," said Sister.

"Come on," said Brother. The scouts followed him into the cave. "Let's just stand here until our eyes get used to the dark. Everybody be quiet and let Lizzy listen."

Lizzy's eyes got used to the dark first.

"Ooh!" she said. "Bones!" Sure enough, there was a scattering of what looked like bones up ahead. Fred investigated.

"Yes!" said Fred. "These could be the fossil bones the professor's looking for!"

"Yuck," said Sister. "Some treasure."

"Hush!" said Lizzy. "I hear voices! I think they're coming from that bend up ahead."

"Follow me and don't make a sound," said Brother.

When they reached the bend they saw something that chilled them to *their* bones. Bigpaw was holding Actual Factual in his big cherry-picker paw. His mouth was wide open and he was looking at the professor as if he were a cherry.

"Here's what we'll do," said Brother in a hushed voice. "Pick up some stones, and on the count of three, start throwing them. Maybe Bigpaw will drop the professor. One, two . . ."

But Brother's voice must not have been as hushed as he thought. Because the professor turned and said, "Dear me! I became so excited about my wonderful discovery that I quite forgot about you. As you can plainly see, our fossil hunt has succeeded beyond my wildest dreams. This cave not only holds the fossil treasure we were seeking, but a far greater treasure: this splendid chap whose measurements I've been taking – teeth, jaws, arm length – that sort of thing. Be a good chap and put me down. I'd like you to meet some very dear friends of mine!"

• Chapter 14 •

A Living Fossil

Bigpaw was much too big to shake hands
with the scouts. But the scouts managed to
shake one of his giant claws. The great
creature didn't have much to say. As each
Bear Scout said, "Pleased to meet you, sir,"
the giant bear smiled a big friendly smile
and said, "Hi," in a deep rumbly voice.

The professor kept on making notes.
"Teeth, about twenty-two centimetres long
– except for the incisors, which are an
amazing forty centimetres long! Gums,
healthy. Nose, cool to the touch . . ."

"Sorry to interrupt, professor," said Scout

70

Brother. "But we're confused about all this. I mean, we came up here to look for fossils . . ."

"And we have succeeded!" cried the professor. "We have found some lovely fossil bones for the museum. But even more exciting, we have found a *living* fossil! As far as I know, it's only happened twice in the

history of science! There was the okapi, an antelope that was thought to have been extinct for hundreds of years, and the coelacanth, a fish that was thought to have been extinct for millions of years. And now Bigpaw! My friends, I can't tell you how exciting this is. Well, if you'll excuse me, I must get back to my measurements!"

"Couldn't the measurements wait, professor?" said Scout Brother. "There's something we're worried about."

"I suppose they can," said the professor. "What's worrying you?"

"Think back, professor," said Brother. "Think back to when Gran predicted Bigpaw was coming. Remember how scared folks got?"

"Yes, I do remember," said the professor. "They became quite agitated."

"Farmer Ben talked about loading up his shotgun," said Brother.

"And Mayor Honeypot said just the

mention of Bigpaw could cause a panic," said Scout Fred.

"You make a very good point," said the professor.

"I mean, *we* know that Bigpaw is sweet and gentle. But he's so frightening-*looking*," said Scout Brother. "When folks see him they'll go nuts! There's no *telling* what they might do."

"You're right," said the professor. "How does this sound as a way of handling the problem? There's a car phone in the Sciencemobile. We'll go back down the mountain and call the authorities."

"You mean like Mayor Honeypot?" said Scout Fred.

"Hmmm, I think not," said the professor. "Panic is the mayor's middle name. No, Chief Bruno is the bear to talk to. He's a sensible fellow and a friend of mine. But first, let me tell Bigpaw we must leave for the moment."

The professor spoke briefly to Bigpaw, then returned to the scouts. "OK, we're all set. Except that Bigpaw enjoyed meeting you and would like to shake hands again."

So, one by one, the Bear Scouts shook Bigpaw's giant claw again. "Pleased to meet you, Mr Bigpaw," said each scout.

"Pleased to meet *you*," said Bigpaw, with a shy smile.

• Chapter 15 •

A Hundred Feet Tall and Eyes of Fire

"Hello, police station. Officer Marguerite speaking."

The police station phone rang often. Most of the calls were about such things as barking dogs, noisy neighbours and accidents. But Officer Marguerite could tell that this call was different.

"Professor Actual Factual, chief. Says he needs to talk to you. Something about preventing a panic."

The chief took the phone. "Chief Bruno here . . . uh-huh . . . uh-huh . . . Well, if you think it's important, professor. I've got some things to do, but I'll be there. Just sit tight."

"What is it chief?" said Officer Marguerite.

"Not something he could talk about over the phone. I've got some business here in town. Then I'll go out and meet him on Mountain Road. Call me on the radio if you need me."

About two miles away, Bear Country's leading crook, swindler and treasure seeker was slowly working his way up the face of Table Rock Mountain. Ralph didn't go in for fancy harnesses and safety lines. He had a simple and direct approach to mountain climbing. He "borrowed" some tree-climbing tools – foot spikes and a climbing hook – while the lumberjack wasn't looking. His plan was to climb straight up Table Rock Mountain by driving in the spikes, then pulling himself up with the hook. It was a pretty good plan, and it might have worked if Ralph had been in better shape. But he hadn't done

any serious climbing since he was a teen-ager back in Big Bear City.

He was getting close to his goal: the cave marked "X". But it was hard going. He'd left a trail of objects all the way down the mountain. The battered brim of his sporty straw hat lay at the foot of the mountain. Its crown was caught on a dwarf pine half-way up. His walking stick had long since clattered down the mountain, frightening the mountain goats. The gold watch he had stolen from a favourite uncle hung on a berry bush.

It had often been said that if Ralph had worked at some honest job half as hard as he did ripping folks off, he'd have been on Easy Street long ago. But like most folks, he was a creature of habit, and all Ralph's habits were bad. He was close to his goal. But the ledge in front of the cave blocked his view. He couldn't see that what was waiting for him wasn't diamonds and gold, but a very different sort of "treasure".

It was now late afternoon. The sun was setting behind the mountains. Bigpaw had come out on the ledge to enjoy the view. There was a chill in the air. Bigpaw decided to make a fire. He did it the old-fashioned way: by spinning the end of a stick in some dry leaves that were placed in a hollow in a larger piece of wood.

Soon he had a great fire blazing. It sent big sparks up into the air. Bigpaw was at peace. As he sat on a boulder, the fire cast a huge dancing shadow on the mountain-side.

That's what Ralph saw when he finally poked his head over the ledge: a monstrous, dancing creature with great floating sparks for eyes. Ralph was so exhausted from the climb that he couldn't tell where Bigpaw left off and the dancing shadow began.

As he sat on a boulder, the fire cast a huge dancing shadow on the mountainside.

Am I losing my mind? thought Ralph. But while he was wondering about that, he lost something much more important: his grip on the edge of Table Rock Mountain!

It didn't take long for Ralph to bounce, rattle and roll down the mountain. By the time he reached the bottom, he looked like the loser in a very one-sided fight. What was left of his clothes was in shreds. What was left of his *underwear* was in shreds.

But did Ralph lie there feeling sorry for himself? Well, he did for a moment. But as he lay there in a heap, one thought filled his mind: *I'VE GOT TO WARN THE OTHERS!*

He leaped up and streaked to town. He broke all records for the two-minute mile. *"BIGPAW! BIGPAW!"* he screamed, as he ran through the town. Ralph was a sight. He looked like he'd been chewed up and spat out. A crowd gathered. The crowd became a mob. Shotguns were loaded. Old cannons were dragged down from the post office steps, torches were lit. Soldiers of the Great Bear War got their musty uniforms out. Swords were drawn. Helmets were dusted. The cry "We've got to get him before he gets us!" went up. The torch-bearing, gun-toting, cannon-dragging mob poured out of town and raced towards Table Rock Mountain.

• Chapter 16 •

A Surging Mob

"They say 'Seeing is believing'," said Chief Bruno. "But even seeing Bigpaw, it's hard to believe what I see."

The chief had met Actual Factual and the Bear Scouts on Mountain Road. He could see Bigpaw up on his ledge from where they were standing. The chief's car and the Sciencemobile were parked side by side.

"From what you're telling me, this Bigpaw – and he certainly is big – saved the professor's life," said Chief Bruno.

"He certainly did," said Scout Sister.

"Scout's honour," said Scout Brother.

"You did right to call me," said the chief. "The news of Bigpaw *could* cause a panic." The police car radio began to crackle. "Wait a minute. Officer Marguerite is trying to reach me." The chief hurried over to the car.

"Look, professor!" said Scout Lizzy. "Something is happening in Beartown. Some kind of crowd, and they're heading this way."

"I really can't make anything out at that distance," said the professor. "I should have brought my binoculars."

"No need for binoculars, professor," said Scout Brother. "Lizzy has super eyesight. If she says she can see something, you can be sure she sees it."

The chief came back. He'd finished talking on the radio and looked very worried. "That was Officer Marguerite. I'm afraid that what we were worried about has happened. A mob has formed and they're heading this way. She says they're armed. They've got cannons, shotguns, clubs, pitchforks, every sort of weapon they could lay their hands on."

The professor pointed towards Beartown. The mob was closer now. They could be seen clearly in the light of the torches they carried. The chief looked through the binoculars he'd brought from the police car.

"Good grief!" he said. "There's the mayor. He's got his old Bear War uniform on and he's waving a rusty sword!"

"This is awful!" cried Scout Lizzy. "It's like an old black and white movie I saw on TV. It's about this giant gorilla they capture and he gets away and climbs a tall building and they shoot him down with aeroplanes. It was awful. I cried."

"Don't worry," said the professor. "We'll think of something."

The mob just kept on coming. When they caught sight of Bigpaw up on his ledge, they slowed for a moment. But then they surged forward again, yelling and screaming.

Of course, Bigpaw could see the mob as well as they could see him. While he was a simple fellow, it didn't take him long to work out that folks with guns and clubs and cannons weren't exactly friendly. He looked around for some way of defending himself.

"Look!" shouted Scout Fred. "Bigpaw's picking up a huge boulder!"

"Can't say as I blame him," said the chief.

"Chief," said the professor. "Do you think those old cannons can reach Bigpaw?"

"Sure," said the chief. "If they don't blow up in the soldiers' faces."

"Oh, dear! Oh, dear! Oh, dear!" cried Scout Lizzy.

In the excitement nobody noticed that Scouts Brother and Sister had left. They had got something out of the police car and were sneaking up the mountain towards Bigpaw.

"How about shooting your pistol into the air?" said Actual Factual. "Perhaps that would stop them."

"Too risky," said the chief. "They'd more than likely shoot back."

"Look," said Scout Fred. "Bigpaw's putting down the boulder."

"Oh, my goodness!" cried the professor. "That's just because he's got a much better idea!"

Bigpaw had reached up and taken hold of the edge of Table Rock.

"Good grief!" cried the chief. "He's strong enough to send Table Rock crashing down the mountain. It'll crush the entire mob!"

"Look!" cried Scout Fred. "They're loading the cannons!"

That was when Scout Lizzy missed Brother and Sister. She looked and looked. But they were gone!

• Chapter 17 •

Bigpaw's Our Friend

"There they are!" cried Scout Lizzy. "Climbing up the mountain towards Bigpaw!"

"They've got something with them!" cried Fred.

"Oh, no!" cried the professor.

Brother and Sister had reached a small ledge just below Bigpaw, who was about to tip Table Rock into the valley. It was clear to everyone that Brother and Sister had done a very brave thing. They had placed themselves between Bigpaw and the mob. If Table Rock came tumbling down, it would be goodbye Brother and Sister.

The mob stopped in its tracks. They stopped waving their guns, clubs and swords. The mob fell silent. In that moment they stopped being a dangerous mob and became a group of individuals worried about the safety of two precious cubs.

What Brother and Sister had taken from the chief's car was a loudspeaker. "You must stop!" said Brother, speaking through the loudspeaker. "Put down your weapons!"

Then Sister leaned over and spoke into the loudspeaker. "Bigpaw's our friend. He's very nice. He saved the professor."

Bigpaw smiled. He stopped rocking Table Rock. Then he reached down and scooped Scouts Brother and Sister to safety.

". . . And now he's saved us!" said Sister. Then she reached up and planted a kiss on Bigpaw's cheek.

A great cheer went up from the crowd. They didn't lay their weapons down. They threw them up in the air along with their torches and hats.

Somehow, the sight of a tiny cub planting a kiss on the cheek of that great monster of a bear told the bears of Beartown how foolish they'd been. They had prejudged Bigpaw. They had decided he was bad before they really knew anything about him. It was a moment and a lesson the bears would not soon forget.

And where was Ralph Ripoff when the great trouble he had caused was happening? He was in the Cuts, Scratches and Bruises ward of Bear Country Hospital. He was checking his new watch against the clock on the wall. He was pleased to find that it was correct.

But Dr Bearden, who had just examined Ralph, was not pleased to find his watch missing. He was sure he'd had it with him – and, of course, he had.

Save That Backscratcher

"That's General Stonewall Grizzwell," said Gramps. "And that other one is General Ulysses S. Bruin. They were the opposing generals in the Great Bear War."

"Yes," said Fred, who read the encyclopedia, as well as the dictionary, just for fun. "I think I've read about them in the encyclopedia."

"I don't doubt it," said Gramps. "Now, come over here." He led them back to Old Shag. He leaned down and brushed the weeds away from the brass plate at the foot of the tree. "All right," ordered Gramps. "One of you read that out loud. And *then* tell me that history's just a bunch of boring names and dates."

"'Old Shag'," said Brother, reading aloud.
"'Generals Grizzwell and Bruin brought the
Great Bear War to an end by signing the
peace treaty under this great tree'."

"Wow!" said Brother.

"Gee!" said Sister.

"Very impressive," said Fred.

"Totally awesome," said Lizzy.

"And then," said Gramps, "they sealed
the bargain by scratching their backs on
the rough bark of this great shagbark
hickory. As did all the members of their
parties: colonels, majors, captains, right
down to second lieutenants."

"It must have been quite a scene," said
Brother.

YOUNG HiPPO SCHOOL

Something exciting is always happening at school in the
Young Hippo School series!

Off to School
Lisa, Ben and Max discover runaway buses, the Big Shirt
Race and a Santa who *takes* presents away!
Jean Chapman

Class Four's Wild Week
Mr Player can't keep up with his class – not because they're
naughty, but because they're too CLEVER!
Malcolm Yorke

Nightingale News
Read all about Jack, Chantelle, Melodie, Owen and
Mustapha's hidden talents!
Odette Elliott

The Grott Street Gang
Something HUGE, hairy and *banana-eating* is about to help
The Grott Street Gang with a dastardly dangerous deed!
Terry Deary

YOUNG HIPPO MAGIC

Anything is possible in these enchanting stories from
Young Hippo Magic!

My Friend's a Gris-Quok!
Alex has a deep, dark secret. He's half Gris-Quok!
Malorie Blackman

Diggory and the Boa Conductor
Why do MAGICAL things happen to ordinary Diggory?

The Little Pet Dragon
James's puppy is glimmering with magic!
Philippa Gregory

Broomstick Services
One day Joe, Lucy and Jackie find *three witches*!
Ann Jungman

The Marmalade Pony
Hannah has always longed for her very own pony...
Linda Newbery

Mr Wellington Boots
Watch out – there's a MAGICAL CAT about!
Ann Ruffell

The Wishing Horse
Albert the horse grants *very* special wishes...
Malcolm Yorke

YOUNG HiPPO FUNNY

Have a giggle with a Young Hippo Funny!

Bod's Mum's Knickers
Bod's Mum has some ENORMOUS and very
useful knickers!
Peter Beere

Metal Muncher
Life's not easy when your baby brother likes to ... *eat metal* !
Kathy Henderson

Count Draco Down Under
Stacey has a strange new visitor – he's a VAMPIRE!
Ann Jungman

Emily H and the Enormous Tarantula
Emily H and the Stranger in the Castle
Emily H Turns Detective
Three funny books about Emily H and her special pet –
Theo, the world's most enormous TARANTULA!
Kara May

Professor Blabbermouth on the Moon
Tonight's the night for Operation Moon Cheese!
Nigel Watts

YOUNG HiPPO SPOOKY

Do you like to be spooked? Then try these!

Ghost Dog
He's big, he's cuddly, he's loyal... he's *ghost dog!*
Eleanor Allen

The Screaming Demon Ghostie
Surely there's *no such thing* as the Screaming Demon
Ghostie!
Jean Chapman

The Green Hand
Dom's new classroom is haunted ... by a Green Hand!
Tessa Krailing

Smoke Cat
Simon keeps seeing something mysterious in next door's
garden...
Linda Newbery

The Kings' Castle
Claude the ghost lives in a castle and likes to cause havoc!
Ann Ruffell

Scarem's House
When humans invade their house, the O'Gools must
SCARE THEM OUT AGAIN!
Malcolm Yorke

·THE KIDS IN MISS COLMAN'S CLASS·

If you enjoy reading all about Karen's adventures in Babysitter's Little Sister, then you'll *love* reading about Karen and her classmates in this new series:

THE KIDS IN MISS COLMAN'S CLASS

ANN M. MARTIN

1. TEACHER'S PET

It's the first day of school, and the kids in Miss Colman's class are really excited – they're going to have a Pet Day! Nancy Dawes doesn't have a pet, but she's more worried that she hasn't got a best friend. . .

2. AUTHOR DAY

Ricky's favourite author is going to visit the school. He can't wait to see if Mr Bennett likes Ricky's stories. Then Ricky makes an embarrassing mistake and decides *never* to read aloud again. Can the kids in Miss Colman's class help him change his mind?

3. CLASS PLAY

Miss Colman's class are putting on a play called *Alice in Wonderland*. Leslie is excited – she *loves* acting. But when Karen gets the part of Alice, Leslie is angry and decides to wreck the show...